Nellie's Knot

For Hogan and James

Copyright © 1991 by Ken Brown

Originally published in Great Britain 1991 by
Andersen Press Limited

Picturemac edition published 1992 by
PAN MACMILLAN CHILDREN'S BOOKS
A division of Pan Macmillan Limited
Cavaye Place, London SW10 9PG
Associated companies throughout the world

ISBN 0–333–56792–7

10 9 8 7 6 5 4 3

A CIP catalogue record for this book is available from the
British Library

Printed in Hong Kong

Nellie's Knot

Written and Illustrated by

Ken Brown

M

MACMILLAN

CHILDREN'S BOOKS

Nellie had tied a knot in her trunk to
remind herself of something very special.
But now she had forgotten what it was! She
tried and tried, but she just couldn't remember.
"I'm not going to untie this knot until I do
remember," thought Nellie.

But a knot in your trunk gives you all sorts
of problems.
"Keep up, Nellie. Keep in line!"
But Nellie couldn't keep in line.

"Don't forget to wash behind your ears, Nellie!"
But Nellie couldn't wash behind her ears.

"Eat your breakfast, Nellie!"
But Nellie couldn't eat her breakfast.

"Catch the bananas, Nellie!"
But Nellie couldn't catch the bananas.

"Blow-up the balloons, Nellie!"
But Nellie couldn't blow-up the balloons."

"Help us put the streamers up, Nellie!"
But Nellie couldn't. She got into a
terrible tangle. Poor Nellie, she couldn't
do anything right, and she still couldn't
remember why she had tied a knot in
her trunk.

"Come and stir the cake, Nellie, and don't
forget to wish!" But, although Nellie
couldn't stir the cake, she *could* wish.
"I wish . . . I wish . . . I wish I knew why
I tied a knot in my trunk!"
But still Nellie couldn't remember.

She went off by herself to have a good, long think.

Then . . . as she was wandering sadly
through the jungle, not noticing where
she was going, she stumbled into a
clearing. All the animals seemed to be
having a party.

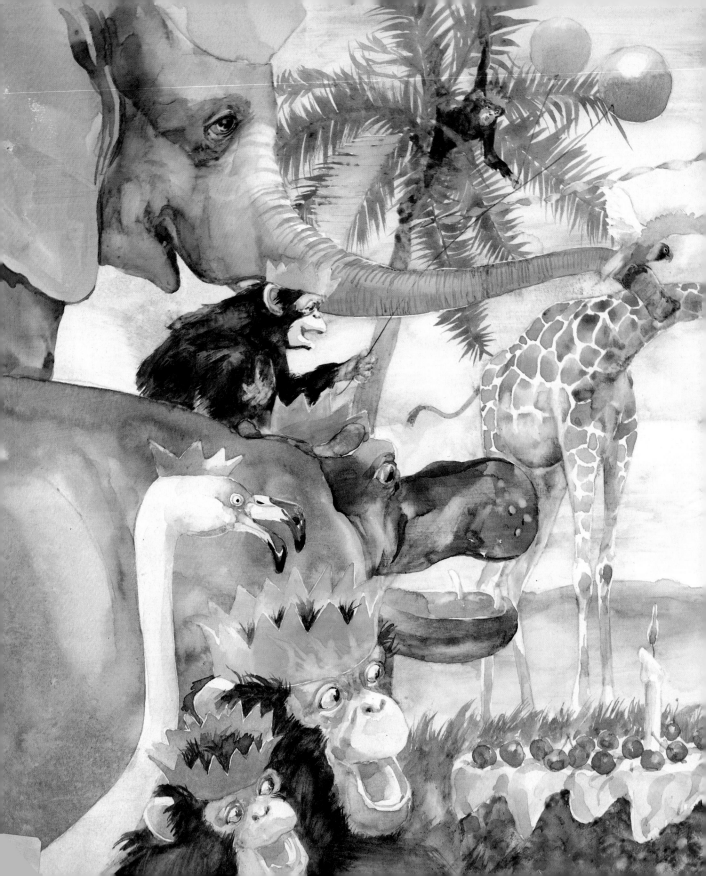

"Come on Nellie! Blow-out the candle!"

Nellie took a deep breath and
blew as hard as she could.
She blew so hard that out
went the candle . . . and
Nellie's knot!
"HAPPY BIRTHDAY, NELLIE!"

Then Nellie's wish came true.
She remembered. It was her birthday!